JOHNNY MUTTON,

MUTTON EAR

MUTTON BRAIN

MUTTON EYE

MUTTON SMILE

MUTTON ELBOW

MUTTON NOSE

MUTTON BELLY

MUTTON SHORTS

Stories and Pictures
by James Proimos

Orlando Austin New York San Diego Toronto London

www.HarcourtBooks.com

First Harcourt paperback edition 2004

The Library of Congress has cataloged the hardcover edition as follows:
Proimos, James.
Johnny Mutton, he's so him!/stories and pictures by James Proimos.
p. cm.
Summary: A kindhearted sheep in human clothing enjoys entering
a cooking contest, planning a birthday party, and participating in a
staring contest, but each event has an unexpected result.
[1. Sheep—Fiction. 2. Humorous stories.] I. Title.
PZ7.P9432Jq 2003
[E]—dc21 2002001573
ISBN 0-15-216760-9
ISBN 0-15-216766-8 pb

A C E G H F D B

The illustrations in this book were first drawn with a pen,
then colorized in Adobe Photoshop.
The display lettering was created by Jane Dill.
The text type was set in Tykewriter.
Color separations by Colourscan Co. Pte. Ltd., Singapore
Manufactured by South China Printing Company, Ltd., China
Production supervision by Sandra Grebenar and Ginger Boyer
Designed by Barry Age

For Ro Stimo

The Stories

3

The Sweet Baby Doll 5000 was Johnny's idea of the perfect robot.

And that is how Johnny Mutton
saved the universe.

The Cook-Off

Mandy Dinkus was a fantastic cook. Well, at least that's what she was constantly telling people.

Then one day Dinkus went too far.

Johnny concocted an elaborate contract
filled with rules, regulations, and cash prizes.
Mandy and Johnny both signed it.

The rules and regulations for the COOK-OFF!

1. Cook something good.
2. Cook it by yourself.
3. Bring it to the park by 2 p.m. tomorrow.
4. Present it to the judges (the Winslow triplets).
5. Winner gets a kazoo, a yoyo, all the change in my shoe box, and the thrill of victory.
6. Loser can't say, "I'm a fantastic cook!" for the rest of her livelong days.
7. Let the fun begin!

Johnny   *Mandy*

Johnny loaded his wagon with cupcakes and headed to the park. But along the way, he met a few folks in need of magic.

14

Mutton arrived at the park just in time to appear before the judges.

Lucky for Johnny, Mandy Dinkus made something so adult the smell alone turned the judges green.

Johnny was happy about winning. But he was even happier about the new friends he had made that day.

Party Animal

It was one week before her birthday, and Gloria Crust was doing her best to get Johnny to plan a party for her.

BOY, IT SURE WOULD BE NICE IF SOMEONE THREW ME A PARTY.

YEAH, BUT WHO?

18

Johnny asked everyone
in class to come.

WILL YOU COME TO MY PARTY?

WELL...

I DIDN'T GET THAT.

WHAT DAY?

NICE SHIRT.

A PARTY, YOU SAY?

I FEEL A COLD COMING ON.

I HAVE A DENTIST APPOINTMENT.

YOU HAVE TO SPEAK INTO MY GOOD EAR.

OH BOY!

Everyone loved Gloria Crust, so naturally they all said they would come.

IT'S FOR GLORIA CRUST!

I'LL BE THERE!

COUNT ME IN!

SHOULD I BAKE A CAKE?

HOT DOG!

A PARTY, YOU SAY!

I FEEL BETTER SUDDENLY!

HOLD ON. MY MISTAKE. I'M FREE THAT DAY!

I HEAR YA, MISTER!

SHE'S MY GIRL!

Mutton was overflowing with ideas for the party all week long. The other kids were not impressed.

Just then Crust showed up. (She was always late.)

Johnny watched her eyes scan the empty room.

To this day, a better birthday party
has never been thrown.

Driving
Mrs. Torpolli Crazy

25

One day Johnny decided he would make Mrs. Torpolli love him. He went to her store and told her so.

TORPOLLI'S

SHEESH.

TODAY I WILL MAKE YOU LOVE ME.

YOU WANT ME TO LOVE YOU? HMMM. PUTTING MR. STOCKMAN'S GROCERIES IN A BAG WOULDN'T HURT YOUR CHANCES.

I'M ON IT, SISTA!

JELLY   JELL

Mutton bagged all that day.
He was awful at it.

LEARN FROM JOHNNY'S MISTAKES.

MR. STOCKMAN'S BAG

DON'T THROW EGGS IN ONE AT A TIME.

LORETTA SMATZ'S BAG

NEVER BREAK BREAD INTO TINY PIECES SO IT WON'T STICK OUT OF THE BAG.

RICO ZANZABAR'S BAG

NO NEED TO TEST THE MILK BEFORE PACKING IT.

VIVIAN BLANKHEAD'S BAG

IT'S SILLY TO POUR KETCHUP INTO THE BAG SO THE LADY WON'T HAVE TO CARRY A HEAVY BOTTLE.

GET OUT AND STAY OUT!

Mrs. Torpolli told Johnny never to enter her store again. She was very angry.

But all that night customers called
Mrs. Torpolli on the phone.

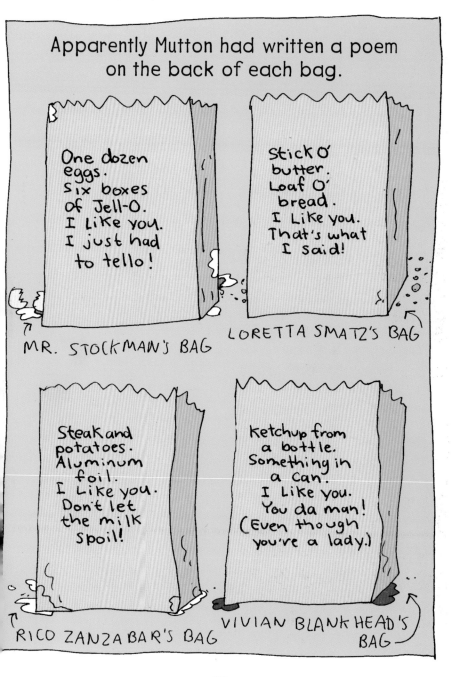

The next day on her walk to work,
Mrs. Torpolli figured out that Johnny
had written all those poems for her.

The Staring Contest

Johnny went on to become President of the World and brought about world peace by instituting "Give-an-Enemy-a-Cupcake Day."

On Gloria's next birthday, Johnny decided to outdo himself and throw her a party that even *he* wasn't invited to.

They Now?

Rico Zanzabar, completely inspired by Johnny's poems, asked Loretta Smatz to marry him.

Rico Zanzabar's broken heart soon mended, and he asked Vivian Blankhead for *her* hand in marriage...with much better results.

Momma won the title
"Staring Champion of the Quad-State Area"
by deploying her secret weapon at just
the right moment.